Red Hawk

The Legend of Red Hawk

R.G. Chur

www.trafford.com
North America & international
toll-free: 1 888 232 4444 (USA & Canada)
fax: 812 355 4082

Titles by R. G. Chur
★★★Dedicated to my sweetheart, Patricia★★★

Rampant River – Civil War novel. (I&R Chur)

Patch – Teen Drug War. Based on a True Story.

English/Spanish Crossover Diccionario – 15,000 recognizable cognates/cognadoes.

Penny the Pink Cloud – Children story, coloring and drawing. Educational.

Crescent Bay – Young Adult novel – 13-17. Football, Surfing, Art, 1st Kiss...

Sugarloaf Mountain Trails – Poems, location Sierra Wilderness.

Sunset Beach – Poems, Pacific southern shores, sea life, sunsets...

Diary of a D.U.I. Victim (D.U.I. Diary) – Chronical of a D.U.I. disaster – facts!

Red Hawk – Flight of discovery over wilderness and sea. Fantasy!

★★★Frances Edenstrom★★★
Illustration Artist
God Rest Her Gentle Soul

★★★Order books through Barnes & Noble, Trafford, Infinity... All major book distributors provide books by R. G. Chur. All titles available on eBook.

Contents

Chapter One

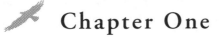

A carrousel of leaves whisked around and around in the autumn breeze. Yellow and gold kites touch, crackle and whirl higher and higher. A young hawk with bright red tail feathers caught the updraft of air and circled the dancing leaves. The hawk settled on the limb of a lofty pine tree.

A robin, disturbed by the intruder, shrieked. "Be still, I sense trouble. Be on guard!" The robin warned.

The hawk searched the forest, a circle of inspection.

"Red Hawk, the storm is trouble and everyone seeks shelter." The robin flew away, searching for more thatch to reinforce her nest.

It wasn't the storm that frightened the hawk. A strange new smell tinted the air. The danger alarm buzzed in the hawk's mind. The hawk lifted into the air and began the search for an answer to the peculiar scent.

The young hawk streaked above the forest floor like a flash of bright red sunlight. Flying through a thick cluster of trees he concentrated on any unusual movement or sound. He sniffed the air.

He flew in an erratic pattern, gliding through the forest, over and under branches, soaring above twisted tree tops. He stalled his flight momentarily and landed on a giant boulder that marked the deer trail leading from the meadow through the forest to the oak grove. His head swiveled left and right, eyes searching carefully for hidden danger.

There was exceptional activity that afternoon in the forest. A mighty storm was approaching, menacing, venomous. The forest inhabitants prepared for the onslaught. The mountain beavers chucked extra leaves and green twigs into their mounds, stashing the food for the stormy days to come. The robin and blue jay selected bits of straw to reinforce their nests. The deer searched for high and dry ground under the giant redwood trees. The rabbits deepened their burrow under the giant boulder.

The forest was alive with warnings. The sound of one excited bird chanting over and over. Quik! Quik! Quik! Another bird cried. Chil! Chil! Chil! Chil! And the whistle of a third, shrill and alarming. Kril! Kril! Kril! All the messages were the same. Hurry! Hurry! Hurry!

The fierce storm was brewing and posed a grave threat to the forest population. Everyone raced against time to secure a safe haven for the night. A black mass of clouds rolled over the horizon.

Gray and white clouds were scattered across the sky like pieces to a giant jigsaw puzzle. Slowly the clouds moved, arranging the fluffy parts into a whole. Slowly a giant black demon was taking shape and pressing down upon the frightened forest.

A chipmunk, busy gathering nuts from under a fallen branch paused, twitched tiny ears and gazed at the hawk. His mate scurried past, chattering a scolding, a warning about the storm. The chipmunks flicked bushy tails and scampered away.

Red Hawk observed the activity without concern. His parents had built the hawk nest high in the giant redwood alongside the mountain cliff. The nest was strong and protected from wind and rain. On this chilly morning his parents left the comfortable nest searching for food. It was not abandonment of responsibility. It was time for the young hawk to become independent and fend for himself. It was the way of nature.

Perhaps the young hawk was overconfident in his attitude. Wicked black clouds smeared the sky. After sunset the storm would descend like a horde of angry demons bent on destruction. Perhaps he should fly to his nest and abandon his search for the strange odor. The wise owl always gave excellent advice. He would search out the owl and seek an answer to his disturbed sense.

Red Hawk lifted gracefully from his perch atop the boulder and soared into the air. He darted through the maze of oak and pine trees and dashed around the towering redwoods. Above the meandering stream, he gazed at the image of his flight reflected in the crystal clear water. Soaring, diving and twisting in flight, the alert hawk followed the stream winding through the forest.

The stream divided at a falls, cascading over a rocky ledge. The left branch of the stream led to the meadow and the high cliff beyond. The right branch of the stream led to the oak grove and the home of the wise and friendly old owl. Since the hawk first took flight, the owl had watched over the young hawk and offered advice and guidance. The hawk choose the stream leading to the oak trees.

His flight through the dense forest was swift and sure. He flew into the oak grove and slowed his flight. He sailed through the grove searching for his friend. The old owl often switched tree locations for his serious meditations and frequent naps.

The wise owl was concealed on the thick branch of a sprawling ancient oak. The young hawk flew to the oak and settled on a branch above the owl.

"Greetings, wise owl. Does the wind bear a strange new smell today?" The hawk twitched his nose.

The great owl smiled a welcome and inhaled the scented breeze. An unknown, powerful odor caught his attention. His keen ears heard strange noises. Swiveling his head, the owl turned his super sensitive ears toward the unintelligible chatter.

"A strange odor and strange sounds." The owl gazed into the distance. He addressed the hawk by the name given because of the unusually bright red tail feathers. "Listen Red Hawk."

The voice of man was heard for the first time by the hawk and owl.

From within the forest sounds held meaning they could not understand. "This secluded valley is untouched. The animals have never seen a man. What a magnificent opportunity to collect trophies."

"We're hunting deer, remember. But not for long, judging the weather."

"What I choose to shoot and hang on the wall is my business."

"Easy Mac! I'm just saying that our first priority is bagging a deer."

"Sure, sure! But, antlers ain't the only prize."

The hawk and owl listened carefully and tried to interpret the alien language. Red Hawk searched the oak grove and spied the source of the strange speech. A long pointed stick was aimed in his direction by a weird creature.

"This telescopic sight is super. Wow! I see a trophy, an old forest owl."

Blam! The sudden sound of death exploded across the forest. The man's dog sniffed the air and bounded forward.

A shot of lead sliced across the old owl's chest; blood speckled the soft gray breast feathers. The owl's burly body catapulted off the oak limb and plummeted in a twisting spiral, down-down toward the mossy bed alongside the stream. The great owl tumbled, falling, falling. A powerful gust of wind caught the owl's wings, corrected the plunge and guided the owl toward earth and the trickling stream flowing around the massive oak.

The great eyes reflected the image of the young hawk. Red Hawk, he thought, his friend. The image blurred and faded. A final prayer for the hawk's safety. A cushion of leaves softened the owl's fall. Blood seeped from the owl's breast and stained the leaves bright red.

Red Hawk stared dumfounded at the fallen owl. The crumbled body of the great bird lay motionless. Another shot exploded.

The sudden sound shocked Red Hawk's sense of normalcy. A chill passed through his heart. The loud, booming sound permeated the forest. The trees trembled. The hawk's ears stung and his vision dimmed.

He flew toward his friend, hovered above the owl's limp form on the forest floor. Gently, gliding downward, Red Hawk settled to the ground beside his friend. A smear of red stained the down that warmed the owl's chest. Red Hawk preened the feathers gently with his beak. Only a warm glow was felt. The owl refused to move.

A red aurora circled the wings of the owl and stained the petals of a crushed buttercup. A trickle of crimson dyed the stream. The golden sand turned red. A thick lily pad was the pillow that cradled the owl's head.

A large gold oak leaf, fluttering, fell beside the old owl. A tiny green frog hop-hopped around the limp wings. A curious crow flew down to investigate. Caw! Caw! It announced its presence and peered at the fallen owl. A humming bird buzzed past and inspected the owl's peaceful eyes.

The breeze fanned the oak branch that shaded the owl. An orange and yellow caterpillar wrapped itself comfortably around a slender twig inches above the owl's head. Stretching comfortably, the caterpillar relaxed and fell fast asleep.

Red Hawk pleaded with the owl. "Fly, fly with me through the sun bright trees. Fly over the forest you love. Fly with me!" Red Hawk understood death. The kill for food or defense. Senseless death defied reason.

The young hawk danced about, fluttered his wings, and demanded the old owl respond. The owl did not respond. A crimson star blazed on the chest of the great owl. The lead bullet had torn a chunk of flesh and feathers away from the owl's breast. A hole pierced the owl's left wing.

A thrashing sound warned Red Hawk of danger. He lifted gracefully into flight. A black beast charged through the forest toward the owl. Suddenly, that same damning sound again, sharp and penetrating. Feathers exploded away from Red Hawk's right wing and he careened downward in an awkward dive.

The body of the old owl softly caught the hawk, breaking the fall. Blood smeared the hawk's feathers. Red Hawk lifted his damaged wing. Two inches of wing dangled from the shattered bone, held together by torn sinew and ripped muscle.

Red Hawk's impact caused the old owl to stir. The owl winked glazed eyes and lifted his head off the water lily. A frog croaked. A butterfly danced off the owl's wing into the air.

"Rise! Rise! Wise owl, rise! A fierce beast strikes." Red Hawk hopped up on a rock.

The huge black animal crashed through the brush to attack the fallen birds. Despite the pain from the tattered wing tip, Red Hawk fluttered his wings and fanned the face of his dear friend.

"Flee! Flee!" Red Hawk screeched.

The old owl ruffled feathers and balanced on shaky legs. His body shook, a wave of dizziness stopped his effort to fly.

The sound of the growl warned Red Hawk. He leaped into the air thrashing his wings awkwardly. The scrap of wing tip dangled and flopped, impeding flight. Appearing out of the dense brush, the snarling black dog, built like a pudgy brown bear, leaped clumsily at the fluttering wing of the hawk. Teeth snapped viciously.

Red Hawk screamed alarm and attacked the charging beast, keeping himself between the snarling animal and the wounded owl. With the one good wing he banked sharply.

The canine teeth closed like a vise. The flapping wing tip was suddenly torn free by the snarling beast.

The old owl rose slowly into the air. Red Hawk doubted the owl's ability to fly far. The howling dog jumped into the air, snatching at the stricken birds.

"I was knocked senseless. I will escape. Fly! Fly! Bold hawk. I will hide in the dense oak with the hollow trunk. You must fly to the cliff. Be swift, Red Hawk."

Balance returned with the loss of the wing tip. Adjusting to the lost weight and wing space, Red Hawk flew awkwardly at first, but then began to glide along the familiar flight path through the bright green leaves of the oak grove.

Looping between two giant oaks gave Red Hawk a moment view of the ugly black invader. His wing tip was clinched between white teeth that formed a grisly smile of death. The hawk glimpsed the owl disappearing between two giant oaks.

The wounded hawk flew around the ancient stump of an oak and two creatures that moved like upright bears came into view. His course through the oaks brought the hawk close enough to the strange creatures to see their eyes confused and amazed. One of the creatures pointed a long, slender sticklike object into the air. Red Hawk dodged through the oak grove. He could hear their confusing chatter.

Blam! A third explosive sound ripped through the forest. "Damn, Butch! Why did you hit my shoulder and ruin my shot? Why'd you make me miss?"

"Look at your dog, Mac."

The big dog dragged the hawk's wing tip through the brush, tearing at the feathers. Boomer was a farm hound and fetched pheasant, rabbit, and squirrel without harm. Boomer knew the hawk and owl were barnyard villains. Boomer thrashed the feathers, steel jaws clamped tightly. Tiny feathers snapped off and limply fluttered to the forest floor.

"One wasted bird is enough, Mac. Your dog tore hell out of your trophy. Forget the hawk and let's get on with the deer hunt. Hunt for a deaf deer."

"Damn you, hound! Drop that bird!" The big man kicked at the dog.

"I told you that dog was worthless on a deer hunt. Old Boomer is okay for rabbits."

"Rotten luck! Damn, Butch, that was a red tailed hawk you made me miss."

"An endangered species."

The strange voices frightened Red Hawk as he fled. He wanted to understand their purpose. Why was the old owl bleeding? If he could only understand!

"Broke my fire! Butch, what a trophy. A red hawk! Damn!" The hunter again aimed his rifle. Red Hawk was at the edge of the oak grove. The hunter took aim, hesitated, aimed again and pulled the trigger. The blast echoed. "Damn! Missed!"

The hawk in flight was a difficult target for his 30-30 Winchester rifle. The lead sphere whizzed harmlessly into the forest. Nevertheless, the additional gunshot boom made Red Hawk increase the beating of his wings, adding speed to his flight.

"I'm not just interested in bagging a pair of antlers, Butch. That owl – stuffed – would have looked great on the fireplace mantel. Butch, that mountain cabin of mine needs interior decorations. And, that hawk sure would make a fine prize, Butch. A beauty! See the red tail feathers. I'll kill that hawk when it lands. Won't that hawk look grand alongside my bobcat trophy? Damn, I'll never forgive you for making me miss that red hawk."

"Mac, I said that hawk is protected by the law."

"Hell, the fish and game department rules by lofty ideals – not facts. The red tailed hawk is over breeding, endangering the balance of nature – breaking down the natural food chain of all the animals of the forest. The red hawk is a pest that kills the pheasant we hunt. And, the red hawk kills the farmer's chickens. There are too many red tailed hawks. Protection be damned!"

"Get caught and you'll pay a stiff fine."

"Hell! I'm willing to take a chance. I want that red hawk beauty. A broken wing tip can be fixed."

The determined hunter sighted through the powerful rifle scope and patiently followed the flight of the red hawk. The young hawk appeared boldly in the cross hairs of the magnified sight. The long blue barrel reflected the afternoon sunlight filtering through the trees. Patiently he aimed, his finger rested on the trigger, ready to squeeze.

Red Hawk could no longer hear the unintelligible language. The hawk flew above the tall, slender pine trees. From his lofty view he surveyed the oak grove. His head swiveled to search the scared face of the cliff beyond the meadow. His keen eyes watched for the intruders.

Despite the pain in his tattered wing the hawk forced his attention on his immediate danger. He must be wary of the strange new creatures in the valley. Was he safe? His nest might be a safe haven for the night, far away from the strange creatures, sheltered from the storm.

Red Hawk remembered the emergency shelter, north beyond the high cliff to the great lake. His father had shown him the lake, a place of refuge in times of danger. At the lake, he would be safe. Red Hawk watched keenly. Perhaps he was safe in his own home. Surely, the cliff was safe. Turning north, he glided over the open meadow.

Before running away he would check the giant redwood hiding his nest. The breeze was stronger and the hawk's flight toward the cliff and the cascading waterfall was hampered. And, with the injured wing and pain it was a slow flight. Across the meadow, Red Hawk flew toward the safety of the cliffs and his hidden nest. He fought the wind while carefully watching for the upright beasts.

Thoughts of the old owl entered his mind. The owl was wise and had taught Red Hawk about life and the great mystery after life ended. No time for such thoughts now. The cliff was near.

Atop the largest cave in the cliff was an ancient twisted old tree extending out over the cave entrance. Red Hawk slowed his flight and perched on the favorite lookout post. The young hawk surveyed the meadow and the forest, looking for movement.

He spied the two strange creatures at the edge of the meadow. One of the beasts pointed a thin stick toward the cliff. Suddenly, that horrible deafening sound shot through the forest, the sound that would haunt Red Hawk's memory forever. The branch he was perched on rocked violently. Wood splinters jabbed into his breast causing needle sharp pain.

The tree branch fell from the cliff. Red Hawk's wings beat the air. The creatures could kill from a great distance like a spark of lightning fire. Flee, he must flee! Rising above the cliff he flew north toward the great lake, but not before a new explosion rocketed through the forest.

Chapter Two

Storm

*M*ile after mile Red Hawk flew above the tree tops. His destination was the great lake deep within the forest. His parents had wisely instructed the young hawk to rendezvous at the lake whenever danger threatened their cliff nest.

It was a long flight and Red Hawk's strength grew weaker. The final rays of daylight dimly penetrated the thick layer of clouds approaching. Halfway to the lake Red Hawk settled on a big rock beside a pool of water fed by an underground spring. He needed to rest and refresh.

Beside him a lizard tensed on the sandy colored rock. The lizard's eyes watched the giant intruder. If it moved the hawk would strike. With luck the lizard might escape with only the loss of an inch of tail. If quick enough!

The open space the lizard must cross magnified the danger of moving to cover. Better to stay tense and wait for the enormous bird to make a move. Safety lay under the thick cluster of roots, leaves and tree bark beside the rock. Better to wait?

Red Hawk dipped his beak into the cool pool of water. The lizard suddenly flashed into motion, scurried across the rock, landed on a familiar bed of leaves and disappeared under the forest debris.

Hawk eyes blinked at the spot the dusty yellow lizard disappeared. He contemplated the disturbance. A likely dinner. The young hawk's stomach rumbled. He would have to be satisfied with water. His first objective was to reach the lake where he would be safe.

Again, Red Hawk sipped water from the pool satisfying his thirst. If he were sure of this place, he would have been splashing playfully in the pool. A lurking bobcat would find his bath amusing. *Best to be wary in strange surroundings,* he remembered one of the old owl's warnings.

An angular green centipede squirmed out from under a leaf and slithered over the forest carpet of moss and pine needles. The young hawk poked a claw at the green centipede. It burrowed under a root. Red Hawk ignored it. He was hungry, and the green centipede looked tasty. Red Hawk knew the insect was poison.

Trees bowed and limbs creaked as the pressure of the wind increased. Five ducks fleeing the foul weather passed overhead, flying in an orderly V-formation. Probably flying to the lake for shelter, Red Hawk determined. He must follow before darkness trapped him by this pool.

Into the sky he rose, awkwardly. He adjusted his flight to compensate for his lost wingtip. Red Hawk guided his flight toward the tiny black ducks in the distance.

Time passed and the sky grew darker. The pale image of the moon flickered in and out of the clouds. Fighting against the powerful new air currents, Red Hawk flew high above the forest. Suddenly, the wind shifted. A northern blast of cold air shocked the young hawk.

Red Hawk circled higher and higher, riding the currents of air around and around, up and up, reaching toward the clouds drifting in the twilight sky. On the northern horizon an immense mass of black clouds churned forward and absorbed the patches of clear sky blocking their path.

The storm would strike before the deep darkness of night, the young hawk determined. The hawk wished he were safe at home in the sheltered nest alongside the cliff caves where the bats lived. Safe in the branches of the mighty redwood, with the old owl nearby for comfort and advice. But, his home was unsafe and the owl hiding. He must reach the lake. Hopeful to rendezvous with his parents.

Red Hawk flew into the wind and approaching storm front. Unfortunately, the wind grew stronger and within the hour Red Hawk was only a mile nearer the lake. A sudden forceful current of air altered his course. He sailed above the dark forest gaining speed. The beauty of the sky and the exhilaration of his flight made him feel alive with joy. Red Hawk gave in to the power of the wind. He allowed Nature to direct his course.

Red Hawk sailed with the wind, captured by the force. The hawk was suddenly hurled upward on a mighty mass of air. The spearhead of the storm! Higher and higher he was carried, helpless to fight the wind that forced his direction. Swiftly the miles passed.

Red Hawk rose high on the updraft, dove on the downdraft, fought for control. He flew between two mighty cloudbanks. Traveling the long alleyway, Red Hawk wondered when the passage would close. When would the clouds press tightly together and squeeze the dense moisture from their mass?

The young hawk flew along the edge of the giant clouds. Hours had passed since the last rays of sunlight had disappeared. Flying blind! Only the bright crescent moon cut into the black clouds like a giant claw. Before the clouds erupt with rain and all light disappeared, Red Hawk must find a safe roost.

A narrow strip of night sky was all that the storm clouds hadn't swallowed. A solitary, bright star glowed on the horizon. The sliver of moon cut a path through the clouds toward a starry heaven.

Below a cold dark forest stripped of trees appeared briefly. A naked bleak swath of charred stumps wound around the mountainous terrain. A grim blackened homeland destroyed by fire. The ugly blackened scenery hurt Red Hawk's heart with feelings of isolation and dismay.

The hawk was trapped high in the sky. Trapped by the swift wind. He was being carried away. Suddenly it didn't matter. It was absurd to try and fight the mighty wind, the will of nature.

At this reckless speed he could only risk a landing on open ground, a meadow or sandy stream bank, the peak of a solitary towering tree. Red Hawk desperately needed to rest. The burnt twisted black tree stumps offered no shelter. His damaged wing ached. His breast throbbed with needle sharp pain. The wind, like a merciless beast, hurtled the young hawk into the stormy night.

Suddenly, Red Hawk heard a roaring monster. The roar sounded above the howling wind. The noise was terrifying.

He realized he must descend. Land blind. The roaring monster must live at the earth's end and would surely destroy everything in its path. Red Hawk must land immediately or parish.

Braking sharply, the wind tore away feathers and tossed him steeply downward. The invisible earth rushed toward him. The roaring sound intensified. Although the earth was invisible, Red Hawk sensed the land's closeness and again braked wings against the wind. A fraction of a second later would have been too late. Red Hawk crash-landed atop a sand dune.

A violent green sea whipped foamy whitecaps toward the sand dune. Waves clashed with the wind and sprayed seawater, drenching Red Hawk. The young hawk's zero dive toward the beach saved him from being carried out to sea by the powerful wind. A blast of sand blinded his eyes, stinging intensely. He blinked rapidly, flooding his eyes with saltwater. He squinted at the sea and beach.

The narrow sand dune bordered the shoreline. The violent sea rushed toward the sand dune. Clusters of rocks were randomly tossed about the beach. The young hawk moved cautiously toward the protective shelter of a cluster of rocks dimly visible.

Red Hawk stood braced against the wind. Eyes rapidly blinked away the flying sand. Wings ruffled and sent out specks of golden sand. Red Hawk's head swiveled left, right, left, continuously searching the strange surroundings. He struggled across the dune.

A giant pine log, tossed over the sand dune by a mighty wave, bashed into the rock pile. Pelted by stinging sand, Red Hawk struggled forward bravely. Cautiously, he moved into the rock and log shelter. The night exploded with bolts of lightning; rain began to fall fiercely. Red Hawk huddled in the shelter and gazed at the angry sea and violent sky. He remembered stories of the sea, the warning by the wise owl – *be wary of mighty waves.*

Stinging sand and cold rain splattered on the rocks and Red Hawk crouched deeper into the shelter. The young hawk peered at the sand dune holding back the roaring monster. Dimly, he could see the edge of the forest. Trees whipped and lashed by the wind. Was it possible to reach the thick green foliage? The wind and blowing sand made any attempt near hopeless. For the moment, Red Hawk was content to watch the passing of the night and to survive. Lamenting the loss of his home and friends, he wept.

The rain beat down and concealed his tears. Millions of droplets striking sand and shells caused a deafening crescendo of sound. A thundering torrent that ebbed and flowed, hour after hour, blotting out the familiar music of the forest and the night. Never had the hawk heard so intense a rain for so long a time.

An old pelican with tattered and drenched feathers appeared out of the howling, blinding storm. The two birds exchanged a flickering blink of shared misery and retreated deeper into the protective cluster of rocks.

"Nobody can fly safely in this storm." The old pelican spoke first. "And, few birds can fly the far sea lanes safely in clear weather." The seafaring pelican stared at the scraggly castaway from the distant forest.

"Are we to be devoured by that roaring monster?" Red Hawk stared at the giant scoop beak and gawky neck of the strange looking visitor.

"That is no monster," the pelican informed. "That's the sea waves thundering upon the shore."

"The raging monster is called the sea?" Red Hawk looked puzzled.

"The sea is a great body of water that is home for many creatures. The sea is no monster. You'll see in the morning, after the storm."

"What terrible roaring." Red Hawk ruffled feathers over his ears. The effort was useless.

"That is the sea's music. Like the waves of the wind. The endless rhythm of the waves. Sometimes the sound is like the gentle swishing of a branch of pine needles. Sometimes the music is thundering like the heavens. The sea is capricious and the sea is endless."

"You speak in riddle."

"Riddle perhaps to the unknowing. Quickly, we must retreat to a higher perch. The sea plays a game with the moon. The tide will sweep away this spot where we stand. Quickly, or we will perish," the old pelican warned.

A wild churning sea tossed forth white-mountains of water that raged and ravished the shore. The thunderous crashing waves rushed toward the rock shelter and drenched the two birds with a salty bath.

"The sea is rising. Quickly, quickly move behind the highest rock." The pelican selected a pathway and carefully weaved between the rocks searching for a safe spot.

Fearful of the strange and wild sea, Red Hawk followed the pelican, grateful for guidance. The young hawk was grateful for the company. The long hours of night passed slowly. A kinship was formed between the two birds after long hours of enduring the fierce storm. The old pelican reminded Red Hawk of his friend, the wise old owl.

"You've eaten enough today, old sea," the pelican admonished. "Go back and play with the moon. Gobble the golden sand of a distant shore. Bother us no more!"

Thunder boomed! Flashing lightning ripped across the black night. Red Hawk shivered violently.

Chapter Three

Sunshine

Fluffy pink clouds drifted slowly along the horizon. The sandy beach became visible, than the waves and the offshore rocks appeared. The new morning sun slowly warmed the earth.

At the first light the friendly pelican said good-bye to Red Hawk and went in search of fish for breakfast. The young hawk watched the gawky looking bird fly over the sea, gracefully sailing above the pounding surf. He watched until the wise pelican was a tiny dot in the sky.

Red Hawk flew up above the beach and circled. Thick white clouds floated close over an ice green sea.

Rain continued to drip from the saturated trees that lined the shore. Streams crackled and churned and rushed to the sea. The forest drank the deep pockets of trapped rainwater. The leaves shimmied, shimmered and shook off raindrops mechanically like a spring recoiling.

For the first time in his life, Red Hawk felt lonely. His surroundings were new and strange. The edge of the forest was shrouded in a mist that stung his eyes. An immense body of salty water, seemingly endless, added to his feelings of aloneness and isolation.

A flurry of wings ruffled the air and a flock of seagulls lifted off the beach. Red Hawk was alone in a world populated by strangers. He must not dwell on his lonely feeling. Loneliness attacked alertness. Combat the feeling! He must become active and find a secure shelter before the return of night. One of the great trees bordering the vast sea would provide a suitable refuge.

Suddenly, Red Hawk's pulse quickened. A walking creature was watching his flight intently. The creature was the female of the strange species with death sticks. Tall, straight, the girl walked alone on the beach, no sign of the fire-stick. The young hawk descended and perched on a giant rock.

Red Hawk's neck swiveled left and right and his eyes winked at each bit of new information. Clumps of kelp grass stretched tentacles in every direction and formed star patterns. Crabs scurried along the base of sea rocks. The eyes returned to the stranger, now standing motionless, watching and waiting. White shells lay scattered around her feet.

"You've had a rough time of it." The tall, suntan girl spoke her thoughts softly. "The storm caught you and brought you here. You're lost and wondering how to return home. Are you bewildered by the strange sights? Sand! Waves! The mighty sea. And, the smells in the misty-salty sea air: fish, giant kelp, sun baked sand – a strange perfume. You are handsome."

Red Hawk's head tucked neatly against his swollen breast. His stout legs held him motionless. A gull cried and flew overhead. Red Hawk screeched and alarmed the timid gull. The walking creature continued to make strange sounds.

"I'll leave you to explore and learn young hawk. May God guide and protect you, injured hawk. Stay free hawk and live long. I would take you home to train, but I see you can manage flight even with that battered wing. You are free and wild. You will survive. Hawk, beautiful hawk, peace."

Lifting lightly into the stiff sea breeze, Red Hawk guided his flight to the nearest and highest tree. Setting on a sturdy limb, the young hawk inspected the land and sea from his lofty view. The hawk felt safe as he watched the girl walk away.

The mighty ocean sound amazed the hawk. The sound was like the wind, constant and weighty in tremor. "The sea breathes in and out with the tide," the old pelican had explained. Red Hawk felt less alone listening to the sea music and remembering his new friend.

Passing overhead a lone seagull cried, calling for companions. The gull veered toward the south and glided along the edge of the forest. A shrill cry echoed again, repeating the lonely signal.

Red Hawk could see the gull's white silhouette against the background of dark trees. A lonely sight, a lonely sound. But soon the gull would find a friend. Unlike the hawk, far from home and friends, facing a strange forest bordering an endless sea. Red Hawk trembled. He must not dwell on the isolation and strangeness. He would control the situation.

Red Hawk was noble and proud of his heredity. The Hawk Family had lived in the forest since the beginning of memory. Individuality and vigilance distinguished the Hawk Family. Red Hawk would survive.

A tiny new robin cautiously poised on the limb below Red Hawk. Before the storm the robin had pondered flight, gaining courage. Now, the robin made the final decision. Launching off the limb, spreading wings, fluttering feathers madly, the robin circled the tree once, twice and disappeared into the forest.

Red Hawk recalled his first flight and the exhilarating feeling of freedom. And, he remembered his home beside the towering cliff. A home so greatly different from the landscape before his eyes. He decided to continue the exploration of this alien landscape. Without hesitation Red Hawk dove from the limb and flew in large circles and increased his altitude until he was a thousand feet above the earth.

Far to the south, he spied a great river flowing into the sea. Red Hawk realized that many rivers were needed to fill so vast a body of water. Two pelicans, following the offshore breeze, glided effortlessly above the wild stormy surf. The young hawk stopped fighting the breeze and followed the graceful wind sailors on their sea voyage.

Below, a dozen dolphins swam in the surf and hunted fish in the morning sunlight. Seagulls hovered above the dolphins, waiting for a chance to snatch at the silvery fish that escape the dolphin attack.

A family of seals played in the tangled kelp forest growing outside the surf. Curling waves washed the rock sculptures lining the shoreline. Red Hawk spied a school of tiny fish flashing in the green sea, but didn't dare attack like the sea birds diving into the sea. He wasn't trained for aquatic hunting.

Red hawk remembered his visits to the great lake. The distant shore of the lake could be seen by flying high in the sky. This body of water was too big to see across no matter how high Red Hawk flew. The young hawk continued his flight along the shore to the rampant river. He descended to see if the water of the river tasted badly like the sea.

The mouth of the river was a graveyard for ancient fallen trees. Bleached bones dried in the sun. Rich verdurous forest colors melted into the sandy rocks and rusty kelp grass.

Red Hawk continued along the shoreline. He lifted higher and higher into the sky, investigating the new and strange landscape. Higher and higher he soared, lifted by the warm updrafts of air. The sea sparkled. The golden beach, speckled with multicolor shells, banked by the lush green forest, ran endless pouring over the horizon.

Gliding lazily on the warm gentle air current, Red Hawk circled higher, sailing further from the land. He spied a great mountain far beyond the forest. The mountain was tipped with white and jutted above the forest a great distance away. Red Hawk looked at the thin ribbon of white surf and shrieked alarm! Without realizing the danger, Red Hawk had drifted far from the shore. Immediately the hawk dived steeply; searched for an air flow to sweep him back to the forest. Unfortunately, a powerful offshore breeze was developing.

What was a new and enchanting seascape a moment ago now became hostile, a death trap. The breeze strengthened and held Red Hawk in check, a stalemate of power. The hawk was unable to make any headway toward the land. Soon the wind would drain his strength and leave his body weak and exhausted. He would plummet into the sea. No! *Think positive*, the wise owl would say. The wind might die or shift direction any moment. The shore was not too distant. He would drift and conserve strength for the flight back to land.

The wind continued blowing offshore, steady and strong, hour after hour. The young hawk, forced to give ground, looked longingly at the tiny jagged line of trees along the horizon. Finally, seeing the line of trees became doubtful. Red Hawk continued to believe he could reach shore if the wind would only stop. "Wind, powerful wind, please, please stop!" The young hawk beseeched the force of nature. The wind mocked his plea with blasts of wind scented with pine.

Weary hours passed. The hawk became dizzy and sensitive to the blinding light dazzling bright on the surface of the sea. He became disoriented and flew at the mercy of the wind. A trick, an illusion in sight. A speck in the corner of his eye. Red Hawk struggled to connect his eyes with thought. Amazing! There was land, yonder.

Land! Land! A speck of land away in the far distance, far out to sea. A speck of land growing in size. An island of land. Red Hawk was saved. Gathering his remaining strength, the young hawk directed his course toward the tiny island.

Chapter Four

Island

*R*ed Hawk screeched excitedly. The tiny spot of land was now clearly visible. A narrow central valley surrounded by low rugged hills. A thin strip of white sandy beach circled the island. Clusters of trees dotted the island, stunted and sparse of leaf. The strong offshore breeze swept him to the north shore, then mysteriously died suddenly.

Three young gulls passed over the strange visitor with the crippled wing. The gulls looked cautiously at the larger intruder. Strong winds sometimes carried forest birds from the mainland. Birds that could not catch food from the sea died. Few managed to survive on the scanty game on the island.

Red Hawk soared high above the island, circling above the beach, watching the far horizon. Higher and higher he soared. Finally, when the island stretched below him in miniature, he gazed toward the land from where he had come. For a moment he thought he could see a very faint line of forest green crushed between the sky and the sea. Then, the ribbon of color disappeared. Did he see the forest or was he seeing a fanciful mirage? He knew the land was far, far away. And, he knew in that instant that he must try to return to the forest.

A sudden gust of wind struck his breast. A cold chill shivered in his heart. Red Hawk had learned his lesson about the fickle nature of the wind. Banking sharply, he descended and flew in a wide circle and inspected his new home.

Along the south shore an old battered pier caught his attention. A puzzling arrangement of rocks and pilings rose from the sea. Two pelicans perched on pillars guarding the abandoned walkway. Seals played hide and seek around rotting pilings that measure the tide.

Descending, Red Hawk landed on a stout piling embedded in the beach sand. Watchful of the hawk, a sea turtle moved cautiously around the pier piling. The young hawk studied the slow, awkward moving creature. A defenseless brute, Red Hawk concluded. The turtle stopped and peered at the hawk perched on the low piling. The turtle's head snaked outward from the shell and the jaws snapped viciously. A fraction closer and Red Hawk's leg would have been crunched in the turtle's vice-like jaws.

Hopping behind the big brute, Red Hawk pecked at the humped body and confirmed his suspicion that it was a hard shell. A pattern crisscrossed the shell and blended with the rocks that were strewn along the shallow surf. A shell to protect and a design to conceal the sea turtle. An ideal home to live and survive. Unlike the hawk who felt inadequately prepared to survive in this strange land. Red Hawk must remain alert if he was to live for long on this island habitation.

The tide crashed against the pilings and submerged the sea turtle. Salty drops of water washed down Red Hawk's feathers. He shivered and for a moment was envious of the turtle's warm, protective shell. The tide pool beside the dilapidated pier was home for the turtle, but obviously unsuitable for a hawk. Although he loved to splash in the cool forest pools, Red Hawk refused this salty bath.

Red Hawk looked toward the tip of the island where the sun was slowly receding toward the horizon. Clouds, like whiffs of smoke, snaked along the ridges and cracks of the low hills. How beautiful the cloud shadows appeared on the wet beach. Clouds floated away over the waves and out to sea.

Night was drawing near. Red Hawk needed to hunt dinner to fill the craving in his belly. And, he needed to secure a place to sleep. Sleep to help cure and refresh his tired and bruised body. The cut wing throbbed pain.

Stiffly, the hawk stretched wings, thrust legs and lifted into flight. He glided gently upon the ocean breeze. Effortlessly, he rose and circled higher and higher. He felt cold and alone above this tiny island world. Survival was the driving force that guided Red Hawk. Instinctively, his keen eyes searched for food and a safe resting place for the night.

So pretty a sky during sunset: white clouds turn pink against velvet blue, scorched with purple flames. Clouds, delicate pink clouds, laced curtains over the window of daylight. Red Hawk looked for the sun's friend, the moon. So tiny tonight, almost asleep, pointing to a new star twinkling light. Peace after the violent storm. A quiet and gently twilight.

Five gulls, then six, three and four more rode the circular air currents upward. White wings glided above the waves that caressed the shore. Nine, seven, five gulls joined together and flew above a sunset, below a field of blue. Ten, twenty, thirty gulls soaring into the sky and riding the carrousel wind higher and higher.

A giant pinwheel ride around and around the tiny island. Seagulls glide, spiral, hover and dive. Angel wings waving peacefully. Around and around. a whirling miniature galaxy.

Red Hawk felt the strong updraft and followed the high flying gulls upward. He sailed past the white gulls, a stranger on the merry-go-round. Another loop, up, up toward heaven. And then, there she was circling above. A hawk, red tail sparked gold, a hawk trapped on the island like himself.

Their circles touched and the pair of red hawks floated past one another, so close as to feel the brush of wing tips and the warmth of bodies. Circling higher and higher almost touching the clouds, now bright pastel colors reflecting the setting sun. A peaceful calm, twilight time. A sense of joy overwhelmed Red Hawk.

The flashing of eyes and love was kindled. Now, the hawk's pattern became a courtship in the sky. A love dance on wings of effortless flight. A wedding of hearts.

Sunlight golden wings stretched outward and she glided and circled. She was beautiful, breathtaking. The hawks soared higher and higher, escorted by the white gulls.

She was grown to full maturity, yet she was frail in stature. The diet of the island was slowly starving her. As they passed a second time, their eyes locked. A new adventure and a new purpose was added to Red Hawk's life.

She made him suddenly aware of his isolation, the loss of friends in the distant forest. How difficult to endure alone this island prison. Red Hawk pushed aside the thought. He was strong, he would endure. He was no longer alone.

The hawks fell deeply in love.

Chapter Five

Trapped

The days passed swiftly. The pair of hawks roamed the island. They hunted in the tide pools and caught trapped fish. Red Hawk learned to crack clams and mussels. He flew high into the air and dropped the shells on the rocks below. Wary mice and rabbits were scarce and difficult prey to catch when found. Few berries or nuts grew wild. The menu was unsatisfactory, survival unassured. Red Hawk hated the restrictive boundary of the small island.

Shallow gray and white layers of clouds covered the morning sky and wept gently. Dark green shadows moved across the ocean. Sunrays radiated through puffs of gray clouds and struck blue flames on the waves. The island colors, sandy reds and rusty yellows, subdued by the filtered sunlight, extended the dawn shadows.

A milky white butterfly, with two tiny black diamonds tattooed on each wing, flutters above the flowers. Red, orange and purple kelp flowers were held by spongy triangular needles creeping across the sand. Golden buttercups danced alongside a bouquet of purple teardrops. Flowers stretched toward sunlight and tasted the morning fogs misty brew.

Red Hawk looked down from his perch atop the round boulder alongside the tiny pool of trapped water, one of the rare drinkable water reservoirs that existed on the island. Another bleak day dawning. A misty gray sky covered the endless sea. A pointless day! Nowhere to explore. Restricted to this island prison.

Red Hawk looked adoringly at his only solace, his mate of destiny flying near, hoovering. The dull morning sun was hiding behind a stunted, twisted ancient pine tree, home for the two hawks. Chalky yellow in the misty morning, the sun slowly, steadily climbed above the horizon. Now, her shimmering red feathers appeared in the pool beneath his perch.

Red Hawk looked at the fleeting image of her beautiful reflection. Her wings flew magically into the face of the pool. Then, she was beside him. A gray field mouse was clutched in her claw. Red Hawk watched her peck at the tender morsel. "You must eat!" She offered him a tempting bite.

Red Hawk declined the food. His attention was attracted to the warring ants beside the boulder. With a slight adjustment of sight, the young hawk focused his vision on the battlefield. Two forces at war. One mound of dirt spewed out pudgy bright red ants with black eyes. The tiny brown opposition ants discharged from the stunted pine trees hollow base.

Large red ants circled around the smaller all brown force of tiny ants. A single brown chain of brown ant reinforcements stolidly marched through the dense green foliage only to be harassed by individual red ant's suicide attacks on the column at random intervals and buried under a mass of brown ants. The brave few brown ants that survived the march to their entrenched comrades were instantly attacked and destroyed by the red enemy.

The brown ants were superior in number, but inferior in size. The smaller brown ants lived in logs and tree stumps. The larger red ants lived in dirt mounds. The brown lancers fought valiantly to their death, killing significant numbers of enemy ants. The battle would continue hour after hour, day after day, year after year. Only the combatants would change as each new generation continued the fight, the cruel conflict handed down by all past warriors. Contested space, the island paradise.

Red Hawk speculated on the outcome of this one battle, but didn't wait for the inevitable end. He lifted into the sky and sent a sweeping wind across the battlefield. He didn't care which ant army eventually ruled this island kingdom. His one wish was to be free of this island. Forever!

Red Hawk circled the battlefield, hardly visible because of the strange stinging moisture that reduced his vision. His companion lifted gracefully from the boulder and followed his flight. Her flashing wings, a single bright silhouette against the empty gray sky.

He had learned that she once lived along the great river that fed the sea. Unlike Red Hawk, she was familiar with the sea and knew the sea stretched forever, an endless journey, a passage to avoid on the path to the Crystal Forest. Red Hawk wondered about his friend, the old owl, and his wisdom about the Land of Forever.

The hawks flew close above the sandy beach. Red Hawk glided above sea waves that indicated a high tide. A gentle breeze flowed along his flight path. Flying parallel alongside was his beautiful mate. Her feathers, speckled with flakes of gold, glistened in the dim sunlight. She had arrived on the island four moons ago. The treacherous storm wind carried Red Hawk to the island. It was a destructive fire that forced her to the island. Trapped in thick smoke and wind she was swept out to sea. Now, the two hawks were together, always and forever.

Red Hawk suddenly veered in front of his mate. "Danger!" He screeched alarm. "Death sticks! Flee! Flee!"

"What is wrong with you, Red Hawk? You act crazy!" The two hawks bumped in the air.

"Death sticks! Flee! Flee!" Red Hawk warned.

She circled the excited Red Hawk. "Nonsense! Fishing poles, harmless."

"Fly away, my love. Quickly, quickly flee! Kill! Kill!"

"No! No! Men catch fish to eat, like the seagulls and pelicans. And, men don't eat hawks. Or I would be a meal long ago. Watch!"

To Red Hawk's horror, she circled and dived toward the boat that carried the fishermen. She was immediately recognized.

"Little beggar. Have a fish. Now go! You have a new lover to follow you around." The old grizzly bearded seaman guffawed. A plump silvery anchovy was tossed into the air. The hawk snatched the fish in her beak and returned to Red Hawk to prove man's innocence and generosity.

So, these sticks were for a different purpose, Red Hawk thought. The poles were used to snatch the fish from the sea.

Food for the upright beasts. The thought made him wonder about the old owl. What was the reason for his friend's blood?

This was no time to speculate on the strange behavior of the walking creature. The white mist was more dense, causing a hazard to flying. This was the eighth consecutive day that the sky became invisible under a thick blanket of fog.

Rolling over the sea, the fog approached in mighty puffs of white mist. Sweeping over the waves, rushing upon the island, the blinding fog cast flickering shadows on the white beach sand. Like the past days, sometimes the fog stayed throughout the light hours and made the hunt impossible.

The hawks subsisted on berries and nuts. Occasionally they dislodged a lizard or field mouse and gouged on the skimpy fare. Red Hawk thought about his vow to return to the mainland and the forest. He often repeated the same conversation with his mate.

"We must leave this island."

"The land is too far."

"No, with the wind right, the land is not too far."

"The flight is too risky. This island is our home."

"We must return to the forest. We cannot exist in this foggy blindness."

"The sun will always reappear."

"We must escape."

The same argument continued. Red Hawk substituted new reasons for trying the flight. But, the fear stopped all purpose and reason. Red Hawk pecked at a strange beetle creature trying to burrow into the sand. He felt like that sand crab. Digging deeper, burying himself in a tiny hole, a cage. Red Hawk felt doomed to this tiny isolated existence. Trapped!

A dark rigid line, barely visible in the fog, marked the low tide line. The line extended across each rock — straight, dark, bold. The sea would soon return to strengthen the line, etch it deeper into the rock. Red Hawk had learned to measure the tide and understand the peculiar changes in the depth of the water. He glanced aloft at the pale shaft of sun in the twilight sky.

The breeze was mild, as was typical in the morning. Red Hawk had observed the changing nature of the winds. It was his determination that with a favorable wind, blowing toward shore, it would be possible to reach the mainland. His thoughts were obsessed with the idea of escape.

Red Hawk's attention returned to the sea and the tide pool beside the old pier. Flip, flop, there was a fish, thin, silver, slick — trapped in the pool. Not the fish of the streams in the forest. The rainbow trout is not like the sea trout. The sea taste is strange. In an instant the hawk stabbed at the surface of the pool and speared the sea trout.

Waves washed the beach, fresh and clean like waves of snow on mountain meadows. Two gulls stood like statues on the pier piling and watched the hawks devour the fish.

Red Hawk looked up at the strange birds and wondered if they were able to fly freely to the mainland. "No gulls return that leave," was the answer when he questioned the seabirds. He had watched the wind and tide carefully. The constantly changing patterns; the random shifts of winds. And the sea, first the high flood, than a low water mark exposing the shoreline. Wind and sea, consistent change. First blowing offshore toward the endless sea. Then, the change and the one chance to escape when the wind blows toward the land.

The wind toward shore lasts hours, sometimes days. And, there were days with no wind. They must begin their flight

when the wind is silent, enough time, maybe. Maybe! Fly
over the sea, hope for still air, fight for the shore, fly, fly,
steadily, conserving strength. If a wind change occurred.
Offshore? Onshore? If? All his thoughts made him realize his
plan to leave the island was a desperate gamble.

They must fly high into the sky, glide and fly straight
toward the mighty forest. Fly high in the air, as high as
possible, until they were dizzy, and the sea was like a blue sky
below. Together they must fly and fly. They must try!

And, if the winds from the forest came to meet them
before the long journey ended, the hawks must fight. The
winds change slowly. They will be well along, more then two
thirds of the way with luck, and no wind or a light wind?
They would be in sight of land. Struggle and fight and we
will succeed.

They must return, now, or never return. They must
leave on the first clear morning. Prolonging the moment
of departure was foolish. Added days with little food will
diminish their strength, destroy their hope of escape. They
must return to the forest, now. They must leave the island
and the endless sea. Next clear morning, Red Hawk decided.
When the wind is silent.

The powerful feeling of confidence overcame the hawk. A
message repeated in his thought – glowing, dizzy, wonderful
message. We will escape! Fly over the sea to the forest. We
will escape!

Chapter Six

Hope

D awn flooded the sea with light. The wind of the night ended. Red Hawk had convinced his mate to attempt the flight back to the forest. Simultaneously, the two hawks lifted off the stunted pine tree. Without looking back, they flew over the rocky beach and out to sea. They directed their flight path toward the invisible shoreline, far, far away. Their future world decided today.

A tight squadron of seagulls flew before them. Hour after hour they followed the gulls until the escort changed direction and circled back toward the island. One high cloud hovered over the island, as if to insure weary sea travelers where land and rest was located.

Red Hawk looked at his companion. She flew gracefully alongside. They were alone in the sky. Was he wrong to convince her to leave the island? Would they escape? Silently,

Red Hawk asked the Great Wind to guide them safely to the mainland forest.

At noon a slight onshore breeze swept them along, steady and gentle as the sun passed the zenith of the sky. The two hawks never veered off their course. Straight and true they flew, maintaining a steady, easy pace. The only interruption to their solitude was the occasional fish that flipped and splashed on the surface of the sea. And, a behemoth shot a jet of water into the sky; the hawks stared, amazed.

Red Hawk guided their flight to a higher and higher altitude. When their strength waned, he wanted the advantage of extra height. Together they would glide downward, conserving energy. Then, gain altitude again and repeat the glide.

It was late afternoon when the breeze shifted and flowed out to sea. The most difficult part of their flight remained. Now, they must fight the wind. Red Hawk believed they were over halfway to shore, but still no land was visible.

The long journey was draining the hawk's energy. And, the flight was now against the wind. Red Hawk began to doubt his decision. Would they fail? The cold blue sea flowed endlessly below.

Red Hawk pushed aside his negative thoughts. They would succeed. They must! Or parish! Fly, fly over the rolling sea. The breeze quickened. Was their direction correct? Red Hawk trusted his instinct and remained constant in his motion, and constant in his determination.

The offshore breeze whistled past and still no land was visible. The two hawks fought errant air currents valiantly. Concentrating on flying, wasting as little energy as possible, they conserved every breath. And yet, it was not enough. Gradually the two hawks separated. His graceful mate was falling behind Red Hawk. He stalled several times to match her weakened pace. Never would he leave her. Never! They would survive or die together.

The sun was now falling toward the horizon. The new moon would soon rise. One last chance. Red Hawk signaled his mate to struggle harder. She was weary, but encouraged by his prompting increased her effort.

It was then that two noble pelican appeared and glided effortlessly beside the hawks. The great sea birds sensed the plight of the strange hawks, but were unable to help. They flew ahead of the hawks, increased the distance between them and they veered south.

Red Hawk understood the importance of observing their direction and altered course to follow the pelicans. Their massive wings stroked the air and propelled the pelicans forward. The hawks attempted to keep pace, but it was impossible and soon the pelicans were distant specks on the dark blue sky.

A great white bird appeared on the surface of the sea. Red Hawk believed it was moving away from the invisible land. And, the creature that carried fire-sticks was manipulating the giant bird. The great bird flew atop the sea waves. Perhaps, the last hope of a resting place on the endless sea. Tired as he was, he knew the risk of the fire-sticks and gained altitude. Away they flew, over the white wings.

Another hour and the day would pass, possibly their last. Summoning reserve strength they fought onward. The wind bit into Red Hawk's feathers, impeding progress. Fear began to gnaw at his thoughts. The sun touched softly the horizon. Twilight descended. Still no sight of land.

Suddenly, his mate screeched wildly. She maneuvered close beside Red Hawk, touching his broken wing tip with her outstretched wing. Her eyes peered at the rising moon. Against the bright yellow moon stood a tiny cluster of towering pines.

Red Hawk looked and increased his speed. The horizon was suddenly a jagged line of tall, forest trees. The trees pointed to the stars like pointy teeth.

Their exaltation was short lived, however. The wind was ever increasing. Before celebrating their return, they must fly many more miles against the powerful wind. Even now, Red Hawk realized that the wind might end their struggle within sight of their destination.

With renewed determination the hawks flapped their powerful wings and advanced slowly toward the distant trees. Very slowly they advanced with great cost to their dwindling strength.

The milky yellow moon rested in the center of the starry sky above the edge of the forest. The last of the sunlight flickered dimly. Bulky white clouds passed over the moon advancing swiftly toward the two hawks. The rhythm of the flight of the hawks was like a powerful drum, wings slapping the air, hearts pumping strong, rapid.

Over the waves they flew. Low and faltering, they flew into the currents of autumn air, across the last mile above the mighty sea. Rolling waves dashed toward the shore. The high cliffs and neighboring hills, rich with color, faded into the darkness. Hope never faded in Red Hawk's heart. Faith in Nature's benevolence.

It was more than surviving the great flight. He was returning with the love of his life. Fate had determined that the two hawks meet. Fate decided to give meaning to his life. They must not parish. His beautiful love carried three new hearts within her, the offspring of Red Hawk!

Now, the shoreline was almost invisible. Two puffy white clouds nudged each other, needlessly maneuvering for space in the night sky. The hawks flew closer together, fearful of losing each other in the deepening night darkness. The wind was a power now. Yet the shore was there, so near. The shore suddenly disappeared on the black horizon. Onward, ever onward. Bravely the two hawks flew into the harsh wind.

Red Hawk peered ahead. All his senses alert. There, he recognized the sound, the wicked monster roaring. And there, a familiar sound, the wind in the forest in the night. With sudden shrill shrieks of joy, they were above the land and flying above the trees. Two wing tips touched and two hearts simultaneously felt the thrill of freedom.

Chapter Seven

Freedom

Wild poppies, bright buttercups, purple pinwheels, green bonnets, blue bells, dandelion puffs. Red Hawk identified the clusters of flowers scattered about the forest meadow. Bright colored petals danced in the gentle morning breeze. Violet, red, gold, orange, yellow, brown – multi-colored autumn leaves danced merrily around the wild flowers.

A thin wisp of cloud hung above a narrow meadow that ran adjacent to the beach. The ocean waves sang a deep throbbing tune. Red Hawk skimmed close to the earth, following the edge of the shadow of the cloud. Almost invisible in the early morning light the hawk hunted breakfast. A pheasant fell prey to his silent attack.

Red Hawk returned to the lofty limb of the great pine and shared his catch with his mate. They chattered about the beauty of the morning and they felt thankful for surviving the flight from the island. Red Hawk gently preened her feathers, golden in the sunlight. He coaxed her closer until two hearts touched. He pecked her lovingly. He knew they would never be separated. He loved her. She loved him.

He had convinced her to leave the island. Now, was she willing to follow him away from the sea? Would she follow Red Hawk deep into the forest to find a new home, a permanent home to raise a family? A home where he would love and protect her always. She seemed to sense his uncertain thoughts and pressed closer. Their conversation turned serious.

"A new home," he ventured. "A home deep in the forest of the far mountain."

"Away from the sea, a shared wish." She snuggled close. "Yes, I will follow you."

"Our new home."

"A home for our family."

Bright sunlight invaded the forest. The two hawks dove from the high perch and sailed away. It was Red Hawk's intent to follow the path of the mighty river, deep inland. He suspected the river might someday reach the great lake near his parents' hidden retreat. Hopefully, he would find his old home safe.

The great river flowed through the burned forest and the lost home of his love. Her parents and forest friends had scattered during the horrible fire. She wanted to see her birthplace and check on her parent's safety. She was frightened of bad news.

From high above the river, Red Hawk took one long last look at the endless sea. The great body of bitter water was quiet this morning. The sea looked peaceful after the harsh days of storm and the long days of fog. Red Hawk was happy to say good-bye. He had struggled with the mighty sea and survived. Now, he must find a home suitable for his family.

It wasn't long before the hawks reached signs of destruction. A blackened, charred ribbon of land snaked through the forest. A wide swath of devastation stretched beyond the horizon and swept east of the river. The landscape was ravaged by the forest fire she survived. They flew over her home site. The blackened destruction was abandoned. No family, no friends, no neighbors, no news.

They flew on and on, deep into the night. Traveling by starlight they flew over the scarred and burnt forest. Only once did they stop to rest atop a giant charred redwood tree. In the morning the hawks flew beyond the charred forest. Her family's fate unknown.

The country inland of the sea was new to Red Hawk. In the night, in the raging storm he flew over this land without seeing. Now, for the first time the hawk saw the marks of man. He spied strange flat dirt pathways, sometimes covered with rock, snaking around the hills. Where did the paths lead? No beast of the forest walked the trail. Red Hawk wondered?

The first building the hawks saw was a white box shape with a pointed spire tall as a young pine – a church, The new noise of a bell ringing. More buildings came into view and the main street of a town. The hawks flew high overhead and gazed at the creations of man. All the sights obliterated by the storm that carried the young hawk to the sea.

Red Hawk observed a number of the walking creatures that inhabited the town. Tiny figures from his great height, but clear. Upright like a bear they moved, like the men that invaded his home and shot the wise old owl. He remembered fleeing his home after the beasts attempts to kill him. No killing sticks were visible. Multi colors of fur covered the strange beasts. The walking animals bumped and passed like ants on a trail.

The warm currents of air lifted the hawks higher and higher. The young hawks veered away and flew northwest until the town was on the horizon. Scattered buildings dotted the countryside. Red Hawk slowed his flight and glided.

The earth below was carpeted in yellows and greens and browns. The icy blue river snaked through the gentle rolling hills and bubbled into small lakes. The river lazily flowed west through the forest to the sea.

The hawk passed over sights he did not recognize or understand. A long black slash that weaved through the forest was a mystery. Nests on logs moved on the flat rock. Old trees bare of foliage and connected by black spider cords, stretched mile after mile alongside the black ribbon. He understood the mystery was connected with the upright creature. A trail for the beast with the fire-stick. A trail to avoid.

From high aloft he saw a field like a giant spider web with scrolls marked by cuts in the earth lined with yellow stalks. It was too uniform for a natural forest meadow. More evidence of the strange creature. The hawks flew deeper and deeper into the forest. At one point the river divided. The hawks chose the left branch, which eventually diminished to a rushing stream. Late into the night they flew and continued flight at first light.

Early in the morning Red Hawk screeched loudly. He recognized the high cliff shielding the meadow from the harsh north wind. He spied the ancient redwood tree, his old home. Beside the old tree was a strange collection of wood. Large logs were pinned one atop the other.

And, the young hawk spotted an animal never seen before grazing on the meadow grass. The gray and white beast had a large nose, almost as big as the moose. Huge nostrils sniffed the air. Large clear brown eyes gazed at the intruders. A shaggy mane graced the long neck. The animal neighed at the hawks, turned and galloped on stout legs with heavy hoofs. As the brute ran, a flashing white tail swished back and forth, back and forth.

A small creature stood in a field. A boy, the child of the man creature. Red Hawk flew lower to observe. The small boy aimed a short stick. A sharp clap sounded and the lead pellet, about the size of a pea, was launched into the air, into the path of the young hawks. To protect his mate he flew toward the boy to block the death from the fire-stick.

Red Hawk felt a sharp pain pierce his breast. The sudden pain was followed by a dull steady ache above his heart. The boy continued to point the short stick, the pellet gun.

"Bang! Bang! Fly away or die, hawk. You can't live here and eat our hens. Flee or I'll shoot again!" The boy aimed his fire-stick.

Red Hawk screeched. "Flee! Flee! Flee!"

"You will not shoot, young man." A woman appeared from the forest. "That hawk has lived here longer than us. You leave the hawk alone. Understand?"

"But, ma! Dad says the hawks eat the chickens."

"More likely the hawks catch rats eating our hen's eggs. Have you seen this hawk kill our chickens?"

"No.!"

"Then you leave the hawk alone. Understand?"

"Yes, mother." The boy frowned and pointed his gun at the ground.

The young hawk flew on, thinking about the boy, the little fire-stick, the pain. Again the sound, a sharp crack, like a tree limb snapping under the weight of snow. And then he thought of his friend the owl and the sound of pain. The sudden sharp sound that stung the ear, louder then the boy's stick, but somehow the same. This could no longer be his home.

The pain continued, and a wave of weakness clouded Red Hawk's vision and caused his flight to lose half the altitude. The tree line was blurred below him. He focused on the beautiful sun-gold wings of his companion before him. He fell into line and followed her flight. Despite the pain, the young hawk was elated to be back, deep in the forest.

The pain intensified. Red Hawk guided his flight toward a giant rock in the center of an open field. The great pointed rock with three smooth sides was a good landing spot. He descended and perched on the peak. A mountain lion paced cautiously across the field. For unknown reasons many cats had disappeared in recent years. A tiny trickle of blood moistened his feathers. For a time he rested and meditated upon the direction toward a new home.

His mate didn't understand Red Hawks sudden descent. It was early afternoon and they never stopped this early. Perhaps this was the place to build a nest, the home to bear their young.

Red Hawk pecked carefully at the tiny hole that seeped blood, and tinted his breast feathers crimson. The pain increased, breast muscle tensed. He continued to probe the wound until his beak touched the hard metallic pellet. Carefully he worked around the lead, gently coaxing the metal to the surface. The tiny ball of lead plinked against the rock and rolled harmlessly to the grassy ground. The wound closed tightly and the pain lessened. Feathers sealed the tear.

Another painful lesson learned about the upright creature. He thought about the future. Never would he allow his

curiosity to take control over his common sense. Despite the
smallness of the walking creature, it was deadly as a tiny viper.
The pain above his heart was a constant reminder of that fact.

His thoughts were interrupted by two chattering blue-
jays. The hawk glared at the intruders and asked pointedly.
"Friendly jays, please tell me. Where is the wise owl that lives
in the ancient oak grove? Where are the great hawks with red
tails?"

The birds cackled hello, answered knowingly. "The
hawks live by the lake. The owl moved south," said the closest
blue-jay.

"Yes, south for health," said the second.

"And south to spread the legend."

"The legend of Red Hawk who saved the wise owl."

"Red Hawk the Valiant."

Red Hawk blinked amazement at his sudden fame. The
hawk thanked the jays and lifted off the rock and again
preceded in a northwest direction. His parents are safe, his
friend safe; Red Hawk felt happy. He flew quickly, and his
mate soared beside him, high over the forest, away to a new
home.

Dipping each wing, they caught the thin drafts of air
and weaved along the narrow pathway of the newest valley.
Memories were flashing back! Red Hawk remembered the
path that the storm had forced him to take. Back across the
high peaks and deep valleys, back toward his home. He
remembered the magnificent meadow and the high cliff, the
redwood giant. The forest where he learned to fly and love
life. The good memories, friends and family. That fateful day
changing his life forever. The death stick!

Day after day they flew. Deeper and deeper they
penetrated the wilderness. Red Hawk reflected that the moon

had twice disappeared in the sky since the great storm swept him into the night and unknown danger.

Now, he was in control. His instincts guided him. He was not held in the clutches of a mighty storm. All his thoughts were positive and directed toward finding a new home to shelter his family. A home! A safe shelter from the winter onslaught. And, safe from the walking creatures with fire-sticks. The two hawks glided forward bravely.

Chapter Eight

Warning

The hawks circled the top of the mountain. An ancient redwood, the top scarred by a lightning strike, stood near the peak of the mountain above a ragged cliff edge.

A second circle, higher, over the rocky barren cliff cut by a rushing cascade of crystal clear water. The rumbling forest stream split and poured into twin lakes.

The third time they circled, Red Hawk made a decision. This would be home. The look of trust in the eyes of his companion reinforced his decision. This mountain was right for them.

The pair continued to circle on the air currents, higher, higher, around and around the great mountain. The hawks gazed below, hypnotized by the panorama of forest life. They flew direct across a meadow, wings expanded to the limit, gliding straight across the lush wild grass, searching for movement in the dense growth. The tracks of rabbit and ground squirrel were visible. Food was abundant!

Red Hawk's eyes scanned the surrounding landscape; he concentrated on his survey. His eyes remained focused, intent, but his heart held the image of the sun golden hawk he followed. The one he loved.

A mature female deer with twin fawns near, bowed when the pair of hawks passed in the sky and acknowledged the birds right to the kingdom above. Noble neighbors in pursuit of the same goals. Family and home, health, happiness, love.

A bumble bee and butterfly sipped nectar from the same giant purple flower. A fluffy orange leaf drifted overhead and skipped around tree limbs. The woodpecker tapped a rhythmic beat.

A rustle of leaves spoke with the wind. The tree limbs embraced and released. The surging stream bubbled and churned, an invisible power. Bright colored pebbles bordered the swift water. Bubbling laughter like chiming flower bells followed the swift stream creating new melodies. The forest trees arched over the friendly water and nodded approval and praise for the songs.

The forest inhabitants gossiped about the new arrivals. "Who were they? Where did they come from? She is beautiful! He is a warrior, see the battle wound. What graceful flying. Will they stay?"

"Ask our friend, the night watch, the owl," Robin red breast suggested.

"Our new friend, friend, friend," chided three red topped woodpeckers.

Three blackbirds in flight glanced dartingly at the hawks as they swerved and banked in the shifting breeze. Butterflies fluttered above the meadow's yellow wild flowers and danced with the slender green reeds. Two busy hummingbirds, buzzing together, acknowledged the hawk shadows.

The day of exploring and settling-in was ending. The moon was full and shinning down on the hawks. The warm body of the sun slipped over the horizon. The blue sky paled. Finally the sun winked good-bye. The moon took over the task of lighting the forest. The hawks settled atop the giant lightning scarred redwood.

Her body snuggled next to his, so warm and soft. She was good to be near. Feathers to touch and caress, playfully pecks. Together they shared a purpose, to renew life. Sleep evaded him. She nestled against him and dreamed.

From the high vantage point Red Hawk watched the moon light the far horizon. The distant trees became stunted, dwindled, disappeared. The brush was split by wider and wider gaps of bare dirt and rock. Flowers and grass, even weeds became scarce. The thick mulch of the soil faded to sand. The forest became the desert. A great divide between wet land and dry land.

Night was closing fast. Stars appeared in the black sky. A quietness settled upon the mountain forest. The swift stream played a gentle melody tonight. The air was occasionally ruffled by a passing wind spirit. The tiny trees swayed, the old trees waved branches. Clouds obscured the moonlight; shadows danced on the forest floor. The hawk's eyes closed the mystic scene.

A sharp pain disturbed Red Hawk's long sleep and tranquil dream. A pain where the lead pellet pierced his breast. He was cautious not to arouse his sleeping companion. Dawn sunrays flickered bright orange rays on the red and gold flakes in her feathers. She remained motionless, breathing contentedly.

Red Hawk dropped from the perch. After a dead fall of twenty feet, he flexed his wings and caught the gentle air current. Red Hawk sailed down from the mountain peak.

The sharp yelp of a coyote pup echoed through the dark silent trees. Tat-a-tat-tat! Tat-a-tat-tat-tat! The woodpecker drilled into the bark searching for a snack before the new dawn light forced the grub deeper into the wood. A wren, gray breast specked with blue dots, deftly snatched a moth from the scattered leaves. A trout flipped lazily from the stream and caught a ray of the sun on silver scales, flashing sparks on fins and tail.

Pink clouds shared the sky with the rising sun. The light of day chased the moon's pale shadow toward the tree-line in the west.

Red Hawk flew in a long arc across the face of the mountain. He glided downward and directed his flight toward the meadow cut by the swift flowing stream. His alert eyes scanned the ground. He searched and recorded every stump, rock, path and movement.

A sight froze the blood in Red Hawk's heart. At the edge of the forest, a man with a fire-stick. And worse, the fire-stick was aimed at the great stag deer that ruled over the meadow.

Red Hawk dived steeply and shot downward like a blazing star. Directly toward the fire-stick he streaked, directly between the bullet and the heart of the great deer. Fearless! An angry young hawk screeched and attacked. Red Hawk's torn wing flashed before the gun sight. The big buck bolted, the hunter fired, the bullet missed. The sound of the fire-stick reverberated harmlessly through the forest.

"What happened, Frank?"

"Don't know! A flash of red light in my sights. The deer bolted. Hell! Don't know!"

"Frank, look, a hawk!" A red hawk!"

The hunter blinked, rested his knee on the ground and braced the rifle. He scratched his head and frowned. "Damn crazy hawk!" The hunter cursed.

It was not to be the last curse aimed at Red Hawk. Other hunters that ventured between high cliffs to hunt near the hidden mountain always returned without game. They told the same story about being astonished by the bold interference of a flaming red hawk that flashed through the sky alarmed any prey, flashed in and out of the rifle sights.

Many hunters stayed clear of the mountain. A legend told of the flaming wings of a hawk that came from the sun to burn the hunter's eye.

As the morning sunrise swiftly passed into daylight, Red Hawk returned to the scared redwood tree atop the mountain. He snuggled against golden feathers, feeling tiny heartbeats. He felt at home. He felt at peace. He felt secure. The glowing sun danced between fluffy clouds. A cry echoed in the wilderness. Red Hawk's cry. Peace on the mountain!

Chapter Nine

Snowball Painting

R.G. Chur

*R*eady! Aim! Throw the snowball at the canvas. Splat! Snowflakes sail. Crystal blue ice shatters on white. Welcome to the art of Snowball Painting.

Artists strive to capture natural beauty. Engaging the substance of nature is inherent to artistic effort. Sculpting wood, stone, clay – the artist intimately interacts with the natural media. The artistic experience is intensified by inclusion of natural methods of application (flint chisel, not chainsaw) in a complemental environment (forest, not studio).

Snowball Painting is an art form exhibiting spontaneity and vibrancy. The art form utilizes a natural condition – cold – and substance – snow – to capture beauty on a controlled space – canvas. Snowball Painting imitates nature's winter art. In nature snow crystals frozen in a pool form a complex abstraction. Light rays ignite colors. An autumn leaf, frozen in ice melt, casts a golden glaze.

Engaging natural components into the artistic mix energizes the composition. Snowball Painting is a way to interact directly with nature to create art. Poetically, the snowball represents playfulness and unpredictability.

Although similar to modern spatter techniques by artists like Pollock, Snowball Painting has uniqueness. The snowball impact creates a burst of color. The effects of ice melting and freezing create unusual designs. Sunrays vaporize snow crystals, imprinting abstractions on canvas.

When the weatherman forecasts snow, prepare to Snowball Paint. The first step to create a Snowball Painting is to select colors. Acrylic, watercolor, poster paints are water soluble, easily mixed and produce quality results on canvas or 140 pound watercolor paper.

What are your favorite colors, light or bold? Color combinations are your choice. Three colors are suggested for your first snowball composition. A combination of blues with a purple works well. Perhaps a fourth color choice – a splash of crimson or pink depending on mood. Experiment. Remember colors will mix because snowballs overlap and blend colors from sun melt.

A small butter dish is excellent for holding paint and will accommodate a fist-size snowball. Plop in the cup two thick globs of acrylic color followed by a shot glass portion of water, mix to a creamy consistency. Add or mix additional color to darken, lighten or enrich. Add white or a color of your selection. Be creative.

You need to prepare snowballs. Fill a bucket with snowballs. Keep the bucket in shade and line the outside of the bucket with packed snow or icicles. Make thirty reserve snowballs in preparation for snowball tossing. Mold various snowball sizes: golf ball size, ping-pong, baseball. In the furry of composition fresh snowballs work best.

Make the snowballs from new sun-softened snow. Snowballs stored overnight turn icy and will bounce off or rip the canvas. Fresh snow sticks together; old snow often crumbles when shaped into a snowball.

Select the time of day for different results. Midday sun melts snow fast. Early evening, crystals melt slowly. Temperature range, 20 – 30 – 40 degrees Fahrenheit, is excellent for Snowball Painting. Painting at zero and below can produce pleasing results. Don't hesitate to Snowball Paint in a flurry of snowflakes.

Attach a canvas to a sheet of plywood with string and nail the plywood to a ground support. A block of wood or log embedded in earth makes a firm pedestal to attach the canvas. The platform should be knee high and level. Be certain the canvas is firmly anchored to the baseboard to prevent a bounce or tilt when hurling snowballs.

Arrange the cups of paint in a convenient location, near the canvas. A dry or wet canvas is the target. Dip a snowball into a cup of paint. Aim and toss the snowball at the canvas. Despite the snowball rotation, the paint side of the snowball will hit the canvas first. Wham – splash! A section of snowball attaches to the canvas, glistening with color. Follow up with a shot of an inky blue snowball. And, a third shot of purple. Aim for a cross mix or single splatter.

To enhance texture add a glob of paint directly to the canvas and smash the glob with a clear snowball or one dipped in white or alternate color. Squeeze paint from a tube on the snowball to create texture. Use colored pencil to create a line design to add dimension or give the eye a point of reference. Designs on the canvas can be created with a string or wire, any assorted shape like a hoop or triangle, your imagination is limitless, like snowflakes – matchless.

After a dozen snowball blasts, allow for melt time and absorption into canvas. Flip canvas to remove excess snow. Your judgment determines the length of time the canvas remains upside down. Allow to partially sun dry or freeze depending on climatic conditions. Develop new techniques.

A second snowball assault is suggested to create a layered effect. Don't be shy with the snowballs, two sets; toss fifteen to twenty-five snowballs. More if needed to cover a square foot space. Partially sun dry the canvas then smash with snowballs a third time and allow the canvas to freeze after sunset.

Learn from experience and experimentation. Tape folded newspaper to the back of the canvas in the frame to prevent snowball bounce. Use a T-Square for maintaining an horizontal focus. Use salt to increase snowmelt and add texture. Add a sprinkle of snow to your paint mix if you're running short in a critical time. Press ice crystals with thumb to disperse chunks of snow. Paper towels are handy to sponge the melt on a strategic color.

Snowball painting produces beautiful color mixes and unusual textures as illustrated on back cover of **Red Hawk**. Watch for visual features in the painting: a face, animal, star, heart. Copy your Snowball Painting to the computer and make a screensaver or winter holiday greeting card. Frame a selection.

Dress warm! Aim true! Think snow! Zing!

Chapter Ten

Game — Mustang Gallop

(R.G. Chur)

GAME INTRODUCTION

From the barren badlands, across desert, rugged terrain, mountain peaks, the Stallion guides the Mustangs to a grazing meadow with a sparkling stream. In Wild Horse Country, a lead horse, Stallion, is followed by the Mustang Herd. Two Stallions will compete for leadership. The pack of horses follow the superior Stallion to the passage to rich graze meadow with water.

OBJECT OF GAME

Two Stallions search for the gateway to the land of plenty (Meadow & Stream win square) leading the wild Mustangs. Every square represents a patch of wild turf absent of water and feed. The faithful Colts follow Stallion commands – White Colt follows White Stallion commands and Black Colt follows Black Stallion commands. The thirteen wild Mustangs obey each Stallion's commands. Mustang movements help determine the leader's progress to the Meadow & Stream square and acknowledgment winning the leadership of the Mustangs.

HOW TO PLAY

1.... Alternating moves, two players determine the best strategy to secure the square designated Meadow & Stream. 2.... The White Colt can only be moved by the White Stallion player. The Black Colt can only be moved by the Black Stallion player. 3.... The Colts are lost and must unite with the Stallion. The Stallion and Colt must touch squares and in a next move switch squares so the Colt will follow the Stallion. Diagonal exchange permitted. Colts cannot land on winning square before a Stallion. 4.... The Stallion leads the Colt and the Mustangs to the Meadow & Stream winning square. All Mustangs can be moved by White Stallion and Black Stallion players. Immediate reversal or redirection of a player's Mustang move by opponent is not permitted.

MUSTANG TOKEN MOVES

1.... No token moves diagonally with the exception of a Stallion touching squares with a Colt of same color. 2.... The Stallions move one space, up/down or sideways like a plus sign. 3.... The Colts moves one or two spaces up/down or sideways like a long plus sign. The Colts can jump over any token. The Colts cannot land on the Meadow & Stream winning square before the winning Stallion. 4.... Frisky Mustangs move one or two spaces up/down or sideways like a long plus-sign. 5.... Stallions can move into a Mustang's square and dislodge two Mustangs of choice – limit two Stallion dislodgements allowed in a game. Dislodged Mustang relocated to barren site of original Stallion square – white or black.

GAME BOARD

1.... The seventeen tokens of Mustangs are arranged on the 56 squares game board (7 by 8 squares) as illustrated on diagram. Traditional checkered game boards symbolically represent destitute land of the Mustangs. Black equals empty land. Red is hot land. Prefer game board of barren brown squares and straw yellow squares. Best token placement on one and a half inch squares. 2.... Location of Meadow & Stream square is indicated by win space on diagram – center square of seven on side opposite Stallion corner positions on board. Colts opposite corners of opposing Stallion. Mustangs positioned on staggered squares.

BEGIN PLAY

1.... Before play begins, flip a coin to select color or start of game. 2.... Play begins with three opening moves in order of positioned tokens shown on diagram. 1st a Mustang is moved by each player. 2nd a Colt is moved by each player. 3rd the Stallion is moved by each player. 3.... 4th and continuing moves by players is random choice of Stallion, Colt or Mustang. Stampeding hoofs guided by Stallion commands. 4.... Mustangs obey Stallion commands to help clear, block or redirect the path to the green pasture. 5....The possibility of a mutual concede agreement to end a game is acceptable. 6.... Develop strategy to distract opponent, focus on goal.

WINNING THE GAME

Remember the pattern to victory involves two steps. 1st Step the Stallion square switch with the Colt. 2nd Step, the Stallion's move to the winning square, gateway to the Meadow & Stream. Two Steps to win the game. The first Stallion to succeed in crossing the 56 square board, shift squares with the Colt, and land on the square leading to the Meadow & Stream wins the game. Have fun! Name your Stallion and Colt. Thunder, Magic, Silver, Shadow, Sundance... Stamp hoofs, charge forward bravely. Gallop!

Game Board – Mustang Gallop

1	BC	1		1	M	1	win	1	M	1		1	WC	1
1		1		1		1	space	1		1		1		1
1		1		1		1		1		1		1		1
1		1		1		1		1		1		1		1
1	M	1		1	M	1		1	M	1		1	M	1
1		1		1		1		1		1		1		1
1		1		1		1		1		1		1		1
1		1		1		1		1		1		1		1
1		1		1	M	1		1	M	1		1		1
1		1		1		1		1		1		1		1
1	M	1		1		1		1		1		1	M	1
1		1		1		1		1		1		1		1
1		1	M	1		1		1		1	M	1		1
1		1		1		1		1		1		1		1
1	WS	1		1		1	M	1		1		1	BS	1
1		1		1		1		1		1		1		1

POSITION OF MUSTANG TOKENS

M represents the position of the Mustangs that Players move by choice.

BS represents the Black Stallion – Moves by only one Player.

WS represents the White Stallion – Moves by only one Player.

BC represents the Black Colt – Moves by only one Player.

WC represents the White Colt – Moves by only one Player.

ATTENTION – SHARED TOKEN MOVES

The shared moves of the Mustangs by both players in the Game – 13 shared tokens – is a unique approach to standard Game Rules. Mustang Gallop with horse tokens of different size and color is the number one competitive illustration of the New Game. However, adaptation of a different game scenario is acceptable. Be creative and select a New Game Theme. Create imaginative tokens. Obey the Mustang Gallop rules for any new theme.

ALTERNATE GAME SCENARIO

Good Spy/Bad Spy competing for the hidden code, rendezvous with a faithful informant and switch squares. Manipulating the patriotic public following the directions from both spies. Spy to reach the informant, exchange squares, and proceed to the code-square wins game.

President/Vice President. Voters engaged to move their chosen leader to the podium for the winner acceptance speech. Switch of square with Vice President, positioning protocol. Coins convenient for tokens. Half/President. Quarter/Vice President. Head or Tail identify President and Vice President. Nickle, dime, penny represent the voters.

Dinosaur competition leading followers from tar pits to safety on the hidden Mesa.

Farm Hounds – faithful farm dogs lead the farm animals – cows, pigs, sheep, donkey – to feed and shelter. Name your favorite team of farm hounds to play. Remember the square switch, one dog jumps forward to the farm gate, one dag falls back to bark and follow.

Prince and Princess Selection. First of the Royal Couples to reach the throne. Prince leads Princess (switch dance squares) to the throne. Thirteen loyal subjects help decide the fate of the Royal Couples. Suggest the couple on top of the wedding cake for Prince and Princess tokens – the perfect couple.

GOOD SPORTSMANSHIP

The Number One Rule of the Mustang Gallop Game is a Friendly Smile win or lose!

Mustang Gallop Game

Biography : R. G. Chur

*M*r. Chur enjoys life with his wife and family. His experiences include college – 200+ units, military and postal service, circus roustabout, racetrack bartender, inner-city teacher (twenty-five years), lexicographer, poet (**Writer's Digest Award**) and novelty artist. Mr. Chur is proud to accomplish nine publications. He is proud of adding 30,000 words to his father's Civil War novel – **Rampant River** – published by Trafford Publishing. Mr. Chur asks his readers to help convince dictionary publishers to identify (underline) English/Spanish cognates/cognadoes in future dictionaries. Also, identify sign language words with a star. Triple language acquisition is achieved in the **English/Spanish Crossover Diccionario** available on e-Book. Recently, Mr. Chur published the **Diary of a D.U.I. Victim** – a diary of his wife's tragic D.U.I. collision. D.U.I. Crime is 100% Preventable.

Description of Red Hawk on Back Cover – The Legend of Red Hawk

*F*ly! Fly with Red Hawk! Imagine the thrill of flight: the hawk view of the world – fury winds, spinning dives, soaring around clouds. Follow Red Hawk, flying above forest and sea. The young hawk, caught by the fickle fate of wind, sails far from home. He discovers the walking creature with fire-sticks. The Wise Owl and Noble Pelican help guide Red Hawk. New challenges test the hawk's strength and skill to survive. Fly with Red Hawk. Fly above the wilderness and reach toward the heavens.

The legend of Red Hawk is sung by the forest birds, heralded by the forest animals, cursed by hunters. **Red Hawk** was written on a solo camp-out in the Oregon wilderness on the old-growth property preserved by Den & Judy Cole, dear friends and dedicated conservationists. The majesty of the pristine forest was inspiring and transcending. The spirit of Red Hawk touches the heart, thrilling the soul.

Enjoy your adventure with **Red Hawk**. Plus, enjoy the new game of Mustang Gallop and create your first Snowball Painting. Guidelines at end of **Red Hawk.**

Printed in the United States
By Bookmasters